It started this morning when a shadow awakened you by flying across your face, silently, wordlessly. The rodent part of your ancestry shook you awake, terrified that you were about to be swooped up. When you looked outside, you saw it was just a crow sitting on the fence. He had positioned himself in the corner of the window so you'd be able to notice him. You wanted to open the window and shout, "What do you want?" but you held on to your question.

In other words, you woke up angry at a crow. And you couldn't get back to sleep with him watching you. You threw off the blankets and got out of bed with a loud stomp.

The next steps were natural. You do them every day. You took a shower. You put on clothes—today, they happened to be all black. And then you ate oatmeal. There was nothing in there that you would've possibly changed.

SPEKTRUM

An hour later at a coffee shop, you were lost in thought and pressing a warm mug to your lips when you thought someone was waving at you, so you smiled and lifted your hand. You didn't recognize this person, but you usually have trouble recognizing faces, and you've decided the best way to deal with this is to pretend like you know them and then figure out their identity through contextual clues in the conversation. The person in the coffee shop looked more familiar than most, but it turned out you didn't know them at all. They were actually waving at someone behind you. Your face flushed, like your body was thinking blood could somehow help this awkwardness. The two people embraced like old friends do, and as you looked at them, you noticed a prism behind them, hanging from the door. It spun a little and the sun had just reached the perfect angle for rainbows to dance around the white walls of the coffee shop.

You thought of the black feathers of crows, that even though they are so black and seem to swallow

SPEKTRUM

all light, they also have shimmering bits of color at certain angles. You thought also of a rainbow you saw on a puddle in a dirt driveway while walking to the coffee shop, and how that is one of the rare times a rainbow means something terrible: some kind of petroleum in the water, the ground-up bones of ancient animals pumped into a vehicle and spilled on the ground.

And then, as you were leaving the coffee shop, you saw it. If the previous things hadn't happened, it wouldn't have caught your eye. It was a flyer with a rainbow on it. That's all. The rainbow caught you. The word at the top of the flyer was *SPEKTRUM*, with a *k*. Some kind of show or art exhibit. It appeared to have been running for a few weeks, and tonight was the last night. It was in a tiny town in the mountains, maybe a twenty-minute drive away. Perhaps this was the first real choice you made all day, to go to this, but at the same time it felt like you had no choice at all. You called the number on the flyer, which seemed like an archaic way to book your place at an event.

"You're in luck," the woman on the other end said. "We've got one spot left."

"Wait," you said. "What is this, exactly? Is it a performance?"

"It's a solo journey," she said. "Your slot will be at 7:45. Make sure you're here early. It's really important."

You couldn't remember it ever mattering whether or not you came to a concert or a play or any other public performance on time. It's not like if you were running late, Tom Petty would silence the Heartbreakers, look out at the audience, and say, "Wait a minute, are we missing anyone?"

"Okay, I'll be there," you said.

And then, every minute after that, you wished you

hadn't booked your spot. You wanted a day without an obligation at the end. Now you would be thinking about this "solo journey."

You had gone to an immersive theater event in New York the year before. They had you put on a mask to conceal your eyes and you got in an elevator with a dozen other people, all wearing masks, and when the door opened, the elevator operator said, "Everybody off." You strode out in that warehouse, the first one off the elevator, and you looked around and saw what looked like the inside of a mental hospital. Long rows of clean white beds. A woman in an old nurse's uniform at the far end of the room, pacing slowly. A string section wailing over the speakers. It felt too intense, all of this emotion. You feel too much in every moment already, like a porcupine with his quills turned inward. You wouldn't have been able to handle such an experience without a dozen other people to share it along with you. You turned around to look at them and—they weren't there.

SPEKTRUM

Nobody else had gotten off the elevator.

Where is everyone?

You felt your brain sweating, the panic of every hair on your head trying to escape, each one exhausting itself to faintness. For a couple seconds you thought that maybe the whole thing was a prank. That everyone was in on it, that this whole multi-floor warehouse immersive theater experience was constructed just to scare the salt out of your cells. And while that amount of collusion would be a terrifying thought, there was also an aspect of that which would be comforting, that so many people would organize something for your benefit, even if it was to scare you. Think of all the planning and forethought that would have to go into such a thing. All for you.

But that experience in New York was ultimately unnerving, and now you don't trust vague performance-art exhibits anymore. It isn't worth it, just for

SPEKTRUM

an experience. There's enough anxiety in the world.

You didn't want to decide whether you would actually go to the rainbow exhibit in the mountains, so you took a nap. You never take naps. It felt like it lasted for hours. You felt more shadows across your face. You woke up, panicked, thinking you had overslept. In fact, you had plenty of time, though somehow your heart wouldn't slow down.

You went outside and found that the glass from a round table in your backyard had shattered. There were no stones around, no dead animals. The umbrella from the table was in the middle of the broken glass, like a great wind had passed through when you were asleep and thrown it like a javelin through the table. Now that you think of it, you had broken two other pieces of glass the day before: one was a wine glass that leapt out of your hands in the middle of a conversation and smashed on the floor, leaving a puddle of Cabernet; the other was a mason jar that jumped out of the cupboard when you opened it, like it was being released from prison.

You drove up the winding mountain road and watched as the houses thinned out and you were engulfed by redwood trees whose giant bodies shadowed you from the lingering light. A few miles before your destination, in the middle of a forest road, there was a red light to regulate the flow of traffic on a section that had only one lane because of an earlier landslide. You eased to a stop and looked at the clock: 7:20. Nobody else was on this highway. You rolled down your window to look at the big lantern, hung above you and glowing red so quietly out there amongst the redwood trees, almost like this traffic light was in a witness relocation program to escape the noisy city and was trying to blend in with its tall red cousins. High up and far away, a hawk shrieked to claim his territory. For a moment it felt that all time had stopped. You inched the car forward to see if it would trigger the light to change. The red stayed illuminated. You peered around the bend, trying to see if anyone was coming from the other direction. The side of the road sloped down dramatically into a ravine. You inched a little more. You couldn't imagine anyone else existing in the world. You inched a little further, and then you sped up and just drove through the red light.

You got into town at 7:30 and parked. Someone let you in through a wooden gate on the side of a dry cleaner's. You asked them if they knew what this was, and they said they had only gotten a call that afternoon to stand there and check people in, and they had no idea what it was all for. You walked through the narrow side alley. Your shirt caught on a nail for a second, stretching the fabric almost to the point of ripping, as though someone were saying, "Wait a minute." As you loosed yourself from that nail, you looked up across the yard and saw another crow inching into place along a power line, like he was being directed by a stage manager. You ordered a vodka cranberry at the outdoor bar, looked at the narrow house, and wondered what was inside.

SPEKTRUM

Now you're here, standing around this fire along with someone named Marissa or Melissa who runs a nonprofit, and Justin—or maybe Travis—who just introduced himself, who works in the Valley. You ask them if they know what happens inside and they say they have no idea. They seem a little nervous, which makes you nervous.

You scratch your right forearm. It has a tattoo in cursive writing that says, "I like your mind and that is all that matters." You pull your sleeve down to cover it. This is your friend Olivia's handwriting. On her arm is the same sentence in your own hand. It's a line from a letter T. S. Eliot wrote to a friend after they had a big argument. You think now of that thing Olivia said to you the previous year as you were recounting the ways that a reluctant lover had been reluctantly loving you. Your arm was crooked over your eyes as you lay on the couch. Your voice was cracking.

Her question: "Are you too cool for God?"

SPEKTRUM

From anyone else in the world, that would have created an uncomfortable situation. You would squirm away from someone trying to save your soul with an old book full of legends. But you know Olivia. Silver threads sparkle in her hair. The night before, she had stayed up until one in the morning counseling a woman a thousand miles away who had called her out of the blue needing help to escape a domestic abuse situation. Helping strangers is the kind of thing she does, every day, for no money. "God" to her isn't a jealous Christian God. It's not a white-bearded man that keeps people in small towns from dancing. It's not the force animating a priest. It's . . . well, you're not sure what it is, but it's not any of those.

Too cool for God. Your first inclination was to answer both yes and no, as if those two words tried to walk through a doorway at the same time, each thinking they were the proper response, hair combed, holding flowers, and then a bottleneck. Yes. No. Yesno.

SPEKTRUM

Now at the Spektrum exhibit, the backyard fire crackles as a voice calls out from the house. The person who you now realize wasn't named Marissa or Melissa but, in fact, *Stephanie* puts down her empty drink and walks in the back door. You can't imagine anything too ostentatious is going on inside this small building. Definitely couldn't fit a roller coaster in there. The door closes, and she's gone. You'll never see her again in your life.

You look at your phone to turn it off and you see a message from a friend asking, "What are you up to tonight?"

Your finger hovers over the keyboard and then you type, "Nothing, but it might take a while."

You add a rainbow emoji, press send, and turn off your phone. You feel like you've let go of the side of a pool in the deep end.

You're a good swimmer, right?

SPEKTRUM

On the movie screen above the bar, the projector shows endless rows of redwoods.

You were in love with longing. That's why Olivia said that to you. You were in love with the distance between what someone says and what they do, as opposed to meeting them where they are. That is indeed a form of being too cool for everything. It allows someone to not participate, to not be present to the real people around them. One tenth of a second after Olivia asked that question, you realized you could have spent your whole life too cool to listen to something other than your own conclusions. You could have easily shrugged all the way into your own grave. You could have even had a clever retort to the psychopomp ferrying you across the river Styx. You could have continued this course of rationalizing, of control, of crossing your arms.

Or you could finally let go.

Justin or Travis has given up on talking with you

and is instead talking with the bartender. You get quiet and press your glass against your lips. A wind rustles through the backyard, perhaps the same beast that broke your patio table earlier in the day.

You take things too far. The accidental wave at the coffee shop. It was just an embarrassing moment, but you had to turn it into a hero's journey. They're about to call you into this house and you still haven't one hundred percent committed to going. You feel the New York elevator moment in your legs again and you realize it's getting dark and cold now, and you could just pretend you forgot something in your car and slip back down the alleyway. You could tell the person at the gate that you'll be right back. You could pat your pockets to suggest that you forgot something. You could jog to your car, get in, and drive away. You could keep your phone turned off so you didn't have to hear the voice of that nice woman asking where you were. You could go home and watch a TV show on your laptop. Something bright and funny, where every pixel dances with a light that tells you you're never going to die. Waves of flickering red, green, and blue, coercing you into a hypnosis. You could get a box of Cheez-Its; you could crawl into bed; you could forget this whole day.

Justin from the Valley is called into the house. He disappears just like the person before him.

You think of the woman on the phone, how intent she was that you be here at this exact time.

"We're so glad that you can participate in this with us."

That's what she said. *Participate.* That's the word that stops you now. An obligation to be a part of something. You picture yourself folding up chairs or sweeping up confetti.

God dammit.

SPEKTRUM

Despite everything, you are here, in the mountains, surrounded by redwoods, standing by a fire. Maybe the crows made you do it. Or the rainbows.

Or that question: "Are you too cool for God?"

This is not God, however. This is art. You don't know what God is. God might just be the center of the gears of the universe that no one is ever able to adequately describe. God might even be those goddamn crows.

You hear your name called, and it feels one-third like hearing the executioner call you up to the gallows, one-third like Mrs. Kozar in second grade asking you to read the writing on the board when neither of you knew you needed glasses, and one-third like hearing a robin singing her familiar song. You remember what happened right after Olivia asked you if you were too cool for God. She saw a ghost on the balcony, and even though you couldn't see it yourself, you were convinced that she was telling the truth. You wished you could see it too, but you kind of understood why you couldn't.

Now you leave the fire pit, put down your empty glass, and walk towards the doorway of the house.

Olivia was terrified of that ghost. Something you couldn't even see at all. She wasn't happy that she could see the dead. She pulled the blanket up to her chin and made a gurgling sound. Her face looked like spoiling milk.

Two people just arrived at the fire as you walk away from it. They say goodbye to you, jokingly, overly dramatic, because they don't even know you. They see a door open, and they see you walk inside, and they see the door close. And they wonder if you're somewhere scary or blissful, if it's dark and lonely where you are. If they'll end up in the same place as you.

∞ ∞

SPEKTRUM

How do I know all this about you? The only part I witnessed personally was when I saw you through a crack in the door as you walked in the side gate and your shirt caught on that nail. It's endearing to see people in those small moments. Sometimes I feel things so strongly it's like I experienced the moments myself.

I appreciate you having the courage to come here. I want to give you some context so you'll understand why I sit here every night waiting for a tea kettle to boil, and why I've hidden myself in a hundred different ways. Sometimes people have to create obstacles in order to get closer to someone. But here I am, sitting, waiting. And there you are, nervous about so many things.

I'll start at the beginning, not just of my life, but my lineage. Trust me, I wouldn't tell you this if it didn't matter.

My sixth great-grandfather Jakub Dabrowiak was

a farmer in the village of Królikowo in what is now Poland. He was born in 1720, was baptized and married in the local church of Saint Vitus, and on a bright February morning at the age of fifty, the earth too cold to take seeds yet, he was walking back from feeding the animals when he collapsed of a heart attack and died in his own field.

There are no written records of my ancestors before Jakub, but, given the slow rate of the spreading of humans across the globe before jet planes, it is likely that many generations of the Dabrowiak family called that same area home. The territories that are now Poland were once the domain of pagans, populated by cults like those that worshiped the *Amanita muscaria* mushrooms, whose ecstatic experiences were converted into Christianity. From the mushroom came the wafer representing the body of Christ. From embodied experiences of love came stories in a book that told about that love. In the year 966 CE, the pagan ruler of those lands converted to Christianity, many gods became one God, and a turning away from wood sprites and relative knowledge began.

Not to say that the turning away was peaceful or natural. It involved violence and coercion and torture, just like any colonizing force does to turn the people away from their land. From fanatic dancing in warrens and dells, from every bush and fog bank representing the breath and expression of a different god in a panoply of spirits, to one man, Jesus Christ. It was the beginning of a new story, one that had never been told before.

The story of the end of the world.

SPEKTRUM

SPEKTRUM

SPEKTRUM

ORANGE

[Drowning people don't look like they're drowning.]

SPEKTRUM

SPEKTRUM

With wood smoke lingering on your clothes, you step into a kitchen. Everything is the color orange except for a man in front of you who is dressed all in white, wearing an apron. He is sweeping the floor when he stops and looks at you. He is wearing a ceramic Day of the Dead mask ringed with orange flowers. You feel icicles up your spine. Your right knee wobbles, always the cowardly part of your body. You think of the elevator doors in Manhattan closing behind you without anyone getting off. You're alone again in the middle of someone else's dream.

You clear your throat, as though you can get the fear out of you that way. As though it's just some cobwebs. There is an old radio on the counter with familiar music coming from it. Hank Williams is singing about someone's cheating heart, or someone's cold, cold heart. A heart gone wrong. A rogue heart. Your shoulders tighten for impact, as though they're preparing for you to launch yourself through the ceiling.

SPEKTRUM

Without saying a word, the man in white steps forward and opens his arms to embrace you. You pause for a moment, one breath in the history of the universe. You're not sure what to do here. You look around to see if there's a route that avoids the hug. He probably opens his arms to everyone who comes in, and more than anything you want to do what's right. Besides, his movements are so light and his gesture so genuine. He's not threatening at all. You decide to just let go a little bit and hug him. It feels like home.

He gestures for you to sit down at the kitchen table. You have a look around as you step across the room. You see that the lightbulb is tinted orange and casting its color on everything in the room. There are thick strings crisscrossing overhead, starting from the eyes of people in portraits that hang on the walls and connecting to other objects several feet away. It's like you've stepped into a loom.

On a shelf you see old tin canisters with flowers on

them. There are a couple wooden alphabet blocks for kids.

You think of the Napoleon House in the French Quarter of New Orleans, the way the paintings were dusty and slightly askew, the way the owner Sal wanted to keep them that way to preserve a certain aesthetic, but he would also still bend down to pick up a piece of lint off the floor so that customers knew the place wasn't a dump.

You sit down. From the radio you hear the Andrews Sisters. The man in white is working at the sink with his back to you. There is a typewritten letter on the table in front of you. Everything about this moment implies you should read this letter. Everything about this day, your whole life, has nudged you into this seat to read this letter. What else are you going to do?

You read it.

SPEKTRUM

Light of the World,

Isn't it funny the way some things choose you as much as you choose them? I chose this place to house my ideas. You chose this place to come spend an evening. So, in some way, we chose each other, like two trees on opposite sides of a boulevard who reach their roots deep underneath and find a way to connect. Even as the world bustles in between us we can still shake hands.

So, we found each other. It feels like a miracle that anyone can find anyone in such a big world. Like hitting a bullet out of the air with another bullet. But if we follow the path to the things that we love, and if we truly love them, it is no surprise when we find each other.

SPEKTRUM

Me, I loved the Big Trees. The
redwoods. I loved the way they stood
for so long, longer maybe than any
other life on Earth. I wanted to see
them, to see the redness of their
skin, to sit in front of them all day
and stare into their bodies, but I
had no way to get over to them. Over
here, where you are now.

I do not want to sound Jealous. I
got to see so many beautiful things.
Walking across the Langebro Bridge
as the sun charted its course for the
day. The streets in Amsterdam, how
they all seem to funnel you where
you wanted to go without you ever
trying to decide where you were go‐
ing. All those proud tulips in the
fields outside Bremen.

SPEKTRUM

To be truthful, I always loved the
chamomile flowers the most. The tisane they make is the most
beautiful golden color. It really
makes one feel like anything is
possible.

Those petals, those little golden
buds.

Here we are again. Were we not here
just a few days ago? Or was it a few
decades? I always thought of Time
as musical octaves, how it spirals
around and how you can be so far
from something and yet so close to
it. I was never much of a pianist,
though I dearly wanted to be. (weep
weep)

I am sorry for tangents. Here we
are again, in the kitchen, where we

SPEKTRUM

spent so many hours in our youth.
All my sincere interests got me
into so much trouble. I really just
wanted to understand myself and
ease the suffering around me.
Funny how threatening that is to
people.

I tried to be an artist. I tried to be
a musician, I tried to be a
philosopher. I was not enough for
any of those disciplines, or they
were not enough for me. I always
wanted to be the spirit animating a
room rather than actually be in it.

One thing I could always do, even
from the very first moment, was love
you. It was so easy. It had more to
do with letting go of resistance
than finding reasons. And that is
true with anything. You just have

SPEKTRUM

    to let go, when you are singing a
note, when you are aiming a sword,
when you are walking through the
forest and looking for the
shimmering leaves of the poppy,
our friend Papaveroideae.

Here is one thing I would love for
you to do.

If you please.

Do it now, because you never know
how much time you have. Write down
on this postcard the name of your
favorite toy when you were young.
Yes, you.

I wanted to live inside a rainbow.
That was my secret dream as a child.
Everyone laughed at me, and I
suppose I understand. It is funny.

SPEKTRUM

The real point is that you must
remember that you are the world's
light, the Light of the World.

    Love, T

The letter feels like a buoy, and now that it is done you are almost afraid to look around again. You forget what *tisane* means. You remember only that it is another word for something common. You wish now you could look things up on your phone.

The man in white sits down across the table from you, though now he has a coyote mask on and no apron. Did you imagine the Day of the Dead mask before? You tilt the letter away from him so he can't see. He has a cloth in his hand and a needle and thread.

You look next to the letter and you see a postcard from Silver City, New Mexico, showing pictures of people on a boat in a lake. *Wish You Were Here,* it says. The back of the postcard is blank. There is a pen next to it.

The man in white stands up and grabs a feather duster and begins to dust something on the wall. He brings your attention to every object he touches, almost like his duster is a spotlight. There is a birdcage, a votive candle, an eggbeater, a vase holding marigolds. In the orange light, the marigolds look absent of color. Not anything on the spectrum, but off it. Not even the opposite of orange. Just . . . well, you don't have a word for it. Just not orange.

You look at the entire length of one of the strings. Close to you there is an old black-and-white portrait of a man and woman. The man is wearing a lumpy suit. His tie is a little askew. She has a black dress with a frilly white collar. What is that thing called? Their shoulders are slouched, like they have carried a heavy weight for their entire lives, and they have dressed up as nice as they can for the one photograph they'll ever take in their lives. These could be your great-grandparents.

The strings cover their eyes. One string from each of these people stretches across the kitchen, connecting to a clock, and the other to what looks like the skull of a calf. The strings are taut, but—and you don't even know why this needs to be said—they are silent.

Okay. Your favorite toy when you were young. This should be a simple question to answer. You can't think of what it would be, though. There is no clear *Citizen Kane*, life-defining response. You're afraid you're going to write the wrong thing. But is there a wrong answer to such a question?

You write, "A stuffed zebra."

You immediately want to cross it off, but you don't. You fold the card in half and stick it in your pocket. The man in white doesn't see you do this.

Billie Holiday is singing "Moonglow," and you finally realize that there is other music beneath the songs from the radio. A drone that is in tune with the music but changing slower. It has subtly grabbed onto your stomach and squeezed it tighter.

SPEKTRUM

You breathe in, trying to extend your belly out as far as it can go. Then you exhale and sit there, seeing how long you can hold it before breathing again. You look at another portrait and see a princess with brown skin. She looks beautiful, but her eyes are covered, so you lose so much about her soul. Her string connects to a book on the shelf. You lean forward and squint your eyes to read the title of it.

The man in white puts down his duster and adjusts his shirt.

Your eyes have acclimated and now you forget what color this room was. Not purple. You think of the color of X-rays. You think of the ghostly reversed image of something that you see after shutting your eyes.

You think of the ghost Olivia saw on the balcony. Now you think maybe you saw something. Your memory puts someone there, like a placeholder. She had a beautiful, lacy dress, that ghost. Like the princess in the portrait next to you. She was clutching something close to her chin.

No, no, that was Olivia.

You redouble your focus on trying to read the title of the book connected to the string. You don't feel like it would be okay at this point to walk over to it. The man in white strides over to the far end of the room. You look at him and see that he stands at a black curtain. You take one last look at the book, but it is too far away.

Bells chime in an ascending melody. You wish you had more time. The man opens the curtain and gestures for you to enter. You don't really feel like you have a choice but to walk through.

∞ ∞

If my sixth great-grandfather Jakub was like half the people alive in Europe in the 1700s, he couldn't read books. But, of course, there are other things to read, like the subtle changes in air pressure, or the bucking of a horse who never seemed to complain before. If you weren't able to read the literal word of God, you would still find it in the trees and the wind, even if you wouldn't dare express such a sentiment in church. Instead, the pastor could read from a wondrous book, and he would shine in his divine connection because of this ability. Supernatural, even, that he could bring to life the stories of people from the distant past, just by reading symbols on a page.

Every book has an end, and at the end of this book was a depiction of the end of the world. Sometimes I wonder where that idea came from. Previously, all the stories were of never-ending cycles, and those stories were still in the fields. The salt, the teeth, whatever was spilled out. Blood, of course, red and darker as it dries, then indistinguishable from the dirt. The knots of the twisting oak trunks, which show, at times, the faces of ancestors, especially when the light dips down to the horizon and shadows pantomime family histories across the brick buildings. Here is a shadow in the shape of someone's grandmother's neck as it falls on the gray cobblestones laid by her father. The trees are pulling the puppet strings, the sun is the spotlight, the fields and the buildings are the stages.

You dressed all in black today. I wonder if you really considered why you did that.

SPEKTRUM

SPEKTRUM

SPEKTRUM

YELLOW

[Play like you are comforting the dying.]

SPEKTRUM

SPEKTRUM

You step through the curtain into a narrow salon.

About ten feet away is another closed curtain. One lamp with a yellow lightbulb paints this room. The man in white has closed the curtain and left to do his work in the kitchen, so you are alone. You think you can hear him open the door to the outside, but you can't see.

You feel like the only thing to do is sit down at this bench in front of a piano.

There is another typewritten letter resting on the piano along with a pair of headphones. You put them on and the drone becomes louder, and the sound of Hank Williams is no longer audible.

SPEKTRUM

Light of the World,

I spent long hours in a salon just
like this with my father. He was
patient, but I think he began to
see in me that I wasn not going to
be like Wolfgang or Ludwig. And
he lost interest. If only there was
more time. Of course, it turned out,
we have all the time in the world,
if we really want it.

First of all, you have your breath.
So do I. That is one thing we have
in common, at least. Also, we both
love music. We are so much the same.

I know you have a tortured history
with this instrument. I have the
same reaction now. I feel the bats
shrieking up in my shoulders. What
has the poor piano ever done to de-

serve this? It just wants to give us
the full light of music.

The Big Trees. I always thought of
them as the slowest animal alive.
They are alive, they are breathing,
they are moving, but slower than
anything you could ever imagine.
What would it take to slow your own
life down to that pace? Even
something close?

The redwoods look like they are
either grieving or celebrating
their ancestors. That is what I
always loved about them. How close
they stayed to home. How much they
revered those who came before them.
Funny for me to say that, someone
who had such battles with his own
father, and who traveled all over
the great continent.

SPEKTRUM

Here is an assignment: Play as though you are playing music for someone on their deathbed. How gentle would you like to play? How important would every note be? Gently! Gently! Like we used to say to old Magnus when he would grab the kittens in his mouth: Gently, dear boy!

Just play. Please. Stay with the white keys. It s okay. You are the best piano player in this room right now.

Play as though you are comforting the dying. Play as though you are the slowest animal alive. Gently. There is never enough time. I will give you time.

    Love, T

SPEKTRUM

Again, you wish the letter would never end because it feels like you're being seen for the first time in a long time. You look above the piano and see a bunch of xylophone bars hanging on strings from a metal rod. They look like a disassembled skeleton in a museum. Above them is a drawing of the solar system, but the planets are all orbiting the Earth, and yet the sun is still in the center. On the top of the drawing it says, "Hypothesis Tychonium."

You almost could have guessed that the letter was going to ask you to play the piano. What else would a letter on a piano ask you to do? But you really don't feel qualified to do that. Even though you're in this tiny room alone, wearing headphones, it doesn't seem like something you should do.

But you look around and realize it's technically true: you are the best piano player in this room. You touch one key to see what it sounds like and it echoes like a flat stone skipping across a pond. Middle C. Where everyone starts.

SPEKTRUM

You remember a piano from your childhood with little stickers on the keys: A, B, C, D, E, F, G, seven notes up the scale like seven colors of the rainbow. Wasn't C a school bus?

When you were a kid, you went to a restaurant called Pizza and Pipes, which had a large dining hall with a man playing a Wurlitzer theater organ. His instrument had hundreds of keys and buttons, some of which would trigger little drums or xylophones sitting on high ledges. In an adjoining room, through big windows, you could see all the brass pipes, standing straight and tall, each one responsible for just one pitch. You would sit on the bench at the dining table and pretend you were the one playing the keyboard. The adults would laugh and point as you went from tier to tier of the invisible magical keyboard, shaking your head as you conducted your own orchestra. You already felt like you knew how to play.

You never did take piano lessons. You only took

keyboard lessons. A relevant distinction in that the lessons occurred in the back of a keyboard shop, and the material you learned wasn't Bach and Chopin, but Prince and Bread.

You got nervous at your one big recital. Something was different in the settings of the keyboard when you started to play. The drum machine was at a slower tempo. Or had your understanding of time changed as you reached this important moment? Regardless, you botched the notes.

Maybe something in the light of this salon makes it seem like this is a do-over. You poke at a middle C again, offering a canary in a coal mine.

And then you play. Like you are comforting the dying.

School bus, school bus, frog, violet.

It sounds like a big responsibility to comfort the dying, but you try to remember how simple it is. Maybe it's like officiating a wedding, in that the purpose is just to be a beacon of love. Remind everyone what they love about the world.

You find a rhythm. You find a melody. You figure it out.

It almost seems like someone's playing with you as you play the piano. The sound is so much fuller than it ever is when you play alone. Maybe this is a magical piano. Maybe a musical ancestor you hadn't discovered is playing with you. You look up again at that diagram of the solar system.

Now, for some reason, you are greeted with a memory you haven't thought about in years.

You were on a side street in Bern, Switzerland one night when you walked past an intriguing man. Possibly because you were next to a clock tower that Einstein used to walk past, you felt like this man was an immortalist or time traveler. You don't know why, but that thought flashed in your head. There was a look on his face like he had been expecting you. You fell into conversation with him without even trying to. He was so curious about your evening, but not in a way that felt like he wanted anything from you.

"Where are you headed in the night?" he asked.

"A dinner party. Up at the top floor of this building."

"A room of people who wait for you. What a splendid feeling. And you are bringing a book?"

There was one under your arm.

"Just in case," you said.

"Of course. I will let you go."

"Thank you."

And then, after you were a step past him, he said, "Will there be time to connect?"

You reflexively said, "Of course," which is the automatic thing you say when you're not sure about something.

"Of course," you said again, but you thought to yourself, *What did he mean by that?*

And also, why would an immortalist or a time traveler ever think there wasn't time enough to do something?

That interaction was so distinct, and yet you can't remember anything about his face. That man could be standing next to you right now and you wouldn't even know it.

Maybe you were wrong about him, maybe it was just a quirk of translation, but you were still thinking about that man a month later in London when

SPEKTRUM

you were trying to fly standby back to the US the day before Thanksgiving. After the last flight left without you, you were staring at Heathrow's monitors when a different man, this one British, was suddenly standing next to you. You told him of your situation.

"Ah yes, you Yanks make such a big deal out of Thanksgiving."

He was funny. Much pushier than the man in Switzerland. You could see this man's age in his tired face. But something of the magic of Bern lingered on your mind when he said you could stay at his house and leave in the morning.

You arrived with him at his house. You can't even remember his name now. His living room was yellow too, and once again, that color seemed to be the product of one lamp. Under that lamp, you saw a framed photograph of the man you were with, which was a funny thing to see. How many people have pictures of just themselves in their own house? On his picture was a sticky note with his name on it and these words:

YOUR SON

You laughed a little at first as you pointed at it, and then you looked at him and saw that he wasn't laughing at all.

"My mum—" he said, and just in that half second you realized what he was going to say.

"—has Alzheimer's—"

You looked around at a living room covered in sticky notes:

LAMP
TV
COUCH

"—and she forgets, you know—"

Suddenly you felt like you were intruding.

"—so I have to remind her who I am."

"Oh. I'm so sorry."

"She's asleep, so we need to be quiet. You can share the bed with me. Is that alright? We can put pillows in between us."

But what kind of barrier is a pillow?

It was too late to find anywhere else to go. This was before cell phones, before easy information. You brushed your teeth, dressed yourself so as to cover up as much skin as possible, and you lay down in your spot against the wall.

Will there be time to connect? You wished, in fact, that time would speed up and you could push past this night.

You stared at the ceiling, hoping he would fall asleep quickly. You thought of your own mother half a world away, and how you hoped she wouldn't fall into such a state of confusion herself. You remembered the last time you saw your own grandmother in a nursing home, and how your mother insisted on trying to get her to remember things. "This is your grandson? Remember?"

And even at that age, you thought, *What's the point of trying to get someone to remember? Who wants to turn their house into a dictionary, always forcing the connection between words and objects instead of letting go?*

And then, in that small bed late at night in London, you thought you felt a hand coming towards you. Impossible to know for sure. It was slow and silent and perhaps it was just in your imagination. Your heart started beating about how stupid you were to get into this situation. Sleeping in an airport while vacuum cleaners moan is not the worst thing to endure for a night. The worst thing would be—

And there it was. A hand touching your thigh. It was unmistakable. It was—

"What are you doing?" you asked in a deep, strong voice.

"I thought," he said, "we could have a cuddle?"

Your heart broke for him, the way he said that word "cuddle," how lonely he must have been in that house with his mom, who constantly forgot his name, forgot he was even her son.

But there was no place for sympathy now.

"No," you said, firmly.

The hand receded. Now you could barely breathe

or move or think too loud, for fear it would remind him that you were there and he would come back for another cuddle. You hoped he would just go to sleep. You wouldn't be able to relax until you heard that unfakeable slow breathing everyone falls into when they're asleep.

You thought of how tired you would be when you got back home to the States. You thought of that hand moving across the bed, how it felt like a shark through water, slow, silent.

Every object in the house stood still. Maybe minutes or hours went by.

Then you felt it. His hand again.

"I'm going to scream," you said. This time your voice cracked a little bit.

"No, please don't," he said, recoiling. "I'll stop."

"I'm going to scream."

"No! Please. You'll wake up my mother."

"Then fucking stop it."

"Okay, I promise."

You exhaled deeply because you didn't know what else to say. What was a promise worth at that point? You hated that you had to use his mother as a hostage, that you pushed at something sensitive like that. But that's part of the bargaining process of the night.

You would wait there, silently, in that bed, through the whole night. You would just not sleep. Any time you felt yourself dozing off, you would shake yourself awake. But as long as you heard the clock continue to tick, as long as you felt the cold on your nose, you knew you were still awake.

SPEKTRUM

Tick.

As soon as there was a little bit of light outside, you'd get up and leave.

Tick.

You'd board the Underground, that train that brings people to all their favorite things.

Tick.

A train that never gets stuck. A train that lifts off the tracks and carries you all the way across the ocean, back home, to a warm Thanksgiving dinner, your mother smiling, the mashed potatoes, the turkey, your uncle laughing, playing Scrabble, the drowsiness afterward, a familiar bed, all to yourself, familiar blankets, familiar ceiling, drifting off, everything safe and warm, your nose finally warm, pillows and pillows and pillows.

SPEKTRUM

You snap into focus. You're alone in a little room playing a piano. You hadn't been thinking about what your fingers were doing. They just found their own way. They rolled like waves. They forgot who they belonged to.

You hear a familiar ascending chime and the man in the coyote mask comes into the room, opens the far curtain, and points you toward the corridor behind it. You feel like you haven't seen him in years. Perhaps this will be the last time you ever see him. You take off the headphones and walk through the curtain.

∞ ∞

That man in the coyote mask isn't me, though he's a friend of mine. He's a wonderful carpenter. He can build a room to whatever whim you give him. Just put together a list of attributes, qualities of light, and he'll put it all in place.

SPEKTRUM

I understand your issues with the piano. I myself have my own set of fears of all those black and white keys. Still, I do much better with music than with things like carpentry, which is strange because I come from a long line of farmers, as you'll see.

Jakub Dabrowiak's son Lukas was a farmer his whole life, just like Jakub, also in the village of Królikowo, which, during his lifetime, became a part of Prussia. Lukas was baptized and married in the same local church of Saint Vitus and died on the same bed where his wife birthed their children, under a quilt his mother made, with his family gathered around him. Candlelight cast shadows on the wall as a pastor took his confessions. Then, the pastor issued the *viaticum*—or last Eucharist—to give Lukas's soul sustenance on his journey, a little wafer meant to symbolize the body of Christ, so that you had him inside you as a guide. The pastor anointed Lukas with olive oil on his forehead and said these words: "Through this holy anointing, may the Lord in his love and mercy help you with the grace of the

Holy Spirit. May the Lord who frees you from sin see you and raise you up." Of course, it was in Polish, so that's just an approximation. When the light left Lukas's eyes, the pastor put out the candle and the family went into the kitchen to have a feast and tell stories.

As a farmer, Lukas had reached the status of *pólkmiec*, which meant that he had attained a fair amount of land through hard work and inheritance, and that land became self-sustaining, as opposed to the lower classes of the commonwealth who were essentially serfs working on someone else's land.

Lukas's son Wojciech, also a farmer, was also baptized and married at the local church of Saint Vitus and died of old age at seventy in a scene very similar to his father, including the last rites, the oil, and the Eucharist.

Wojciech's son Jan was a farmer, too. He too was baptized and married in the local church of Saint

SPEKTRUM

Vitus and died coming home from that same church one day at the age of fifty-nine. A horse was nipping at his coat when someone finally came by and noticed the body.

SPEKTRUM

SPEKTRUM

SPEKTRUM

HALLWAY

SPEKTRUM

SPEKTRUM

You walk through the curtain and into a hallway. There are portraits on the wall with fancy frames around them, as though you are now in a Hall of Fame. One of the portraits is of a man from several hundred years ago who kind of looks like a walrus, with a big, long, blond mustache. He is dressed in black velvet with one of those white, frilly, air filter–looking things around his neck. What are those called? Not a cravat. A spoiler? No, that's not it. He is also wearing a thick chain that holds a brass pendant of an elephant over his heart. The man's eyes look weary, like he has seen everything you could possibly want to see. No, there's more in his eyes. He's looking slightly to the side. If you posed for a painting back then, you'd be very deliberate about your facial expression, because you'd have to hold it that way for a while. Why would he give *that* look?

The hallway turns to the left and you see more portraits of elaborately dressed people from long ago. Maybe this was back when scientists were considered alchemists. They all look like they swallowed a

SPEKTRUM

certain amount of mercury.

Next to the portraits are written all kinds of equations. In the middle of them, there is a drawing of a circle circumscribed by a square, which is circumscribed by a triangle, which is circumscribed by another circle. There is a green door at the end of this hallway that is slightly ajar. A number is painted on the glass above the door: 135711.

On a little table next to you there is a book with a red cover. Your first thought for some reason is that it is the book from the kitchen that was too far away to see. On the cover it says S P E K T R U M. You pick it up and flip to the middle. For some reason, that's where the copyright page is. Maybe this is a misprinted copy.

It says:

SPEKTRUM

For Chelsea

SPEKTRUM was constructed on the unceded lands of the Ohlone and the Awaswas-speaking Uypi Tribe, in what are now called the Santa Cruz Mountains. It was built by Sarah Farrell Mackessy, James Mackessy, and Nick Jaina, to the specifications of an anonymous European benefactor.

Special thanks to The Magic Chipmunk Caballeres Quilting Circle for invaluable curatorial insights about the nature of color, space, and time: Betzi Jackson, Minna Jain, and Cori Storb.

Thank you also to Olivia Pepper, Joshua Rose O'Hara, Nathan Langston, Pamela Vasquez, Bernardo Paz, Emily Coletta, Adriane White, Terry McCants and Chelsea Coleman for their insights.

Additional editing by Adam Prince
Copyediting by Esa Grigsby
Genealogical research by David Nowicki

S P E K T R U M

Published by Modern Mythographer Press
Emeryville, CA

© 2022 Nick Jaina

S P E K T R U M/ Nick Jaina
ISBN: 979-8-218-03080-3

All rights reserved. No part of this book may be used or reproduced in any manner without written permission from the publisher, except for brief quotations in reviews.

Second Edition May 2023

nickjaina@gmail.com
www.nickjaina.com

Printed by Ross Newport
Community Printers
Santa Cruz, CA
and set in Georgia, Alchemist, and 1651 Alchemy

SPEKTRUM

SPEKTRUM

SPEKTRUM

GREEN

[We have seasons because the Earth tilts slightly. Is there anything in your own tilting that brings the opportunity for Spring?]

SPEKTRUM

SPEKTRUM

You push open the door and suddenly you're outside.

Or it feels like it's outside. There are vines on the walls, and everything has that negative ionic feeling of nature. It's amazing that after only a few turns in the hallway, you have no idea which direction you are now facing.

As you take a step, you see a woman with black curly hair sitting at a table. Her long skirt almost reaches the floor, and her bare feet are poking out. All about her is the scent of roses. A bouquet of them is on the table. Rosewater glistens in the air. Also on the table are a couple of crystals and a braid of sweetgrass.

You sit down in front of her, and she smiles as knowingly as you've ever seen someone smile. Friendlier even than those people greeting each other at the coffee shop.

She says, "I remember when you were a baby."

You breathe deep and sink into your seat.

"This is a room where things are going to happen that no one will know about," she says.

This could sound like a threat, but these are the most loving words a stranger has ever said to you. She called this a room, so you must not be outside, but everything is so lush and green. She looks like she's been tending a garden all day and just stopped to gaze at you with all the love and devotion of leaves stretching towards the sun.

"Do you have a postcard?" she asks.

You do. It's in your pocket. You pull it out and unfold it.

She takes it lovingly and reads it out loud.

"A stuffed zebra," she says and smiles. She holds it to her chest like it's a gift just for her. "That is so wonderful."

You feel bad because you wrote that down in haste and now it seems to mean so much to her. You almost want to apologize, to say that you can change your answer. She looks at the words, still smiling. Then she tears the postcard apart and puts the pieces on the table. She puts her hands over yours.

"I want you to remember all the things you loved about the world."

Okay, yes, that sounds good. You will remember. Of course, you will remember.

Wait. Did she say *loved*—like, past tense?

You notice this is the first room without a letter waiting for you, but it doesn't matter. This woman is everything you needed from the letters. Maybe the letters were from her. You take another deep breath and think about what you love about the world. You close your eyes.

You think first of trees. The way there are so many of them, and they don't demand to have their own individual names, like Steve and Tracy, and they are just collectively so overwhelming when they whoosh past you as you drive on the winding roads through the forest. You always feel like you don't have enough time with the trees, that you should stop your car and read a book under each one. But what are you talking about? They're trees. There's always time to connect.

You want to tell this woman about the time you spent a night next to a grizzly bear without realizing it. That image just popped into your head, and now your heart is beating fast because you want to talk about it. It wasn't scary, that moment. It was just curious and joyful, like this moment now.

You open your mouth to say something. Maybe she's still thinking about the stuffed zebra. But she ripped up the card, so perhaps it doesn't matter.

"There was—" you start, but every word feels like a whole book to say. Your voice has no volume. But not because you're scared.

She smiles and closes her eyes, like she already understands everything. But you want her to understand more.

"I wanted—" you say.

She opens her eyes.

"—more time."

She nods and smiles.

It was in Denali National Park in Alaska, where

the grizzly bears have had such well-managed interactions with people that those encounters aren't dangerous. Not that any of your friends ever believed this was true. You always wanted to tell them that flying in a plane, driving in a car, and eating the Western diet was more dangerous. Then you stopped trying to convince everyone of what was safe and what was dangerous.

"Bear," you manage to say to the woman holding your hands in the green room.

She looks you in the eyes and listens like no one ever has before.

But the words are beside the point. You want to tell her about the procedure for dealing with a grizzly bear in Denali: First of all, if he hasn't noticed you, just leave him alone. Keep at least three hundred yards of distance between you and the bear. Absolutely do not run. If the bear does see you, make yourself look big, and yell something. You had settled on the phrase, "BEAR! BEAR! BEAR!"

When you actually saw a bear, out there all alone, far from any cabins, fences, or any structures at all, he was far enough away that you backed up into the aspen trees before he saw you. You listened for the bear approaching, but you heard nothing. Your heart was beating fast. You looked up at the sky and figured there was maybe an hour of light before it got dark. You saw fog start to fill in around you. An owl flew slowly, silently, right overhead. You prepared yourself for a big burst and then you crashed through the aspens shouting, "BEAR! BEAR! BEAR!"

But you didn't see the bear. Was he gone?

The northern lights were so beautiful that night. And there you were, Orion the hunter, with the three stars of your belt. You were still while the waves of light moved through you, like you had a fixed purpose, like your role had been cast ages ago and was set for millennia.

You woke up at dawn the next morning and unzipped your tent. Everything had a light dusting of frost on it. You stood up and started to put your boots on. Your eyes were a little blurry. You kicked some frost off your laces and bent over to tie them when, about thirty feet away, the grizzly bear poked his head up from a gully.

Ho-ly FUCK, you thought to yourself as you stood up straight.

You were mutually surprised that you had both spent the night so close to each other. He had a bit of frost on his head. You took an extra second in this moment, face-to-face with a grizzly bear. He looked genuinely curious, not aggressive in the least. You knew you were supposed to shout at him to scare him off, like the film in the visitor center had told you to do. But that was for legal reasons, right? They didn't know the majesty of standing there in the presence of an actual bear. They couldn't imagine what kind of mutual mischief you could get into together.

What did you love about the world? You loved that it was so real. That you honestly didn't know what was going to happen from one moment to the next. That nothing was for certain, even your own life. You loved the little facets of the mountain, and how they changed as the sun crossed the sky. You loved the bushes that at first, in your excitement, looked like bears. You loved that you always had to try.

You wanted to dance with him. You wanted to spend the day walking around with him looking for berries. Can you job shadow a wild animal? You wanted to hunt him. With plastic arrows. Just for fun. To put on your ancient costumes. To track him through wilderness for days and days. To sneak up on him, try not to step on any branches, and shoot at his heart. And if you missed, it would be trouble.

But mostly you wanted that moment alone with the bear to stretch out longer. Just to be the closest person in the world to such a creature. You knew you had to yell. You knew you had to put on that coat of armor and that belt and become the Hunter.

You raised your hands over your head and shouted, like you were reciting an old college fight song, "BEAR! BEAR! BEAR!"

He looked disappointed. Like your mother had told you you weren't allowed to play with him and he didn't want to accept it. He took one step to walk away and then looked over his shoulder to give you another chance.

You redoubled your efforts and yelled, "BEAR! BEAR! BEAR! BEAR! BEAR!" like you were emptying every bullet in the chamber on him. He gently turned and walked away.

When you were back at the visitor center later that

day, you were suddenly inside the fenced part of the world, and everyone talked so loudly and their zip-up sweaters were so clean, and you found your brain starting to relax in the safety, knowing that you didn't need to keep scanning the horizon for danger. Now you realized that's how things are named. In your vigilance, a rock looks like a bear from far away, and then you walk up to it and call it Bear Rock to feel safe. You wanted to hold onto that feeling of attentiveness, but there were a bunch of signs with words on them, there was a vending machine selling candy bars, and there was just no way to stay in that mindset.

In the green lounge now, holding hands with this woman, you cry. You wipe your tears with your sleeve. You cry for everyone who honestly tried to get you to see something that you refused to see, for all the times you didn't try harder.

You realize that you've only said the word "bear" to her and then cried for several minutes. That's all you could manage for the person who was listening more intently to you than anyone ever has.

You look down at her arm and see these words:

"I like your mind and that is all that maters."

You feel goosebumps on your arm. You don't have time to ask about it. The bells chime again and a different woman emerges to escort you out. Like the man in the kitchen, she is dressed all in white with the addition of a veil. She gestures you to follow her. You don't want to leave, but you have no choice.

∞ ∞

I will try to speed up my part of the story. I'm trying to cover centuries and you're covering minutes. I hope to meet you at the perfect time.

Jan's son Nepomucyn was born in 1861 in that same village of Królikowo and was baptized in the same local church of Saint Vitus. But when Nepomucyn was eighteen, something extraordinary happened, as bizarre a thing as if you suddenly were ejected into outer space to begin a new life: he took a ride on a steamship from Europe across the ocean to Philadelphia, Pennsylvania, where the name *Dabrowiak* was first recorded in the United States. He never went back to Poland. Whether that was heartbreaking, triumphant, or somewhere in between, it is hard to say, because census records only mark the transitions of a life and don't gauge how people feel about them. Nepomucyn finally settled in South Bend, Indiana, and went by the name John. He lived until 1928, when he disappeared while traveling to a nearby town in the winter. There was some confusion about which town he'd been heading to, so his body was only found weeks later, outside a factory. No one knows what happened. In his long life, he had traveled farther, faster, and experienced more technological change than all his ancestors combined, but when I feel for him in my chest, he's in the cold, all alone, and terrified.

SPEKTRUM

SPEKTRUM

BLUE

[Waves and frequencies become
overwhelming in their accumulation.]

SPEKTRUM

SPEKTRUM

The woman in white is with you for just a few seconds. She leads you to a little booth where you sit down and put on noise-canceling headphones. Then she's gone. A blue light is cast across the small space. In front of you is a little device with four clear dials on it, several black letters written on each. The shadows of the letters are projected on the wall, and you can spin the dials to change what they say in whatever way you want.

As you sit down, the shadow letters read:

L E A D

You're not sure if this is *lead* like the metal or *lead* like the opposite of follow.

There is a piece of paper sitting on the table. You recognize the words "Light of the World" like it's your own name. It's much shorter than the other letters you've read.

But you don't want to read it yet. Instead, you close your eyes.

You remember a song. You haven't listened to it in probably two decades, but now you remember it clearer than the music in the kitchen.

"Sweet Jane."

The simple, slow guitar chords. The hi-hat.

You only know about it from the cover version in that movie about serial killers. Jane knew it from the Velvet Underground. You grew up in a house without vinyl records. Her name was in the title. Of course she would know about it.

You were always two steps behind Jane. You wanted to meet her in the place she was, but you kept wilting and she kept drinking. The only place you could truly have met her would have been at the bottom of the ocean. You tried to get down there, but you were too buoyant. Your body rejected the poison. It's as if your parents sewed water wings into all your clothes.

You heard the song in that wobbly, underwater shimmer: "Anyone who's ever had a dream." That was you. You had a dream. A dream to be adored, to be heard.

She drove you places in her white Rabbit. The meaning was too spot-on, that Volkswagen would manufacture a car with that name and offer it in white. You rode in the passenger seat as the car filled with tea rose and cigarette smoke.

And so, your role models became serial killers. Just for a moment, and not for their killing, but for their audaciousness, their romanticism. You came to believe that true love could only happen in the midst of chaos. Maybe you needed police looking for you to have your vibrancy validated. This might have been in response to the very non–serial killer love your parents had for each other. You wanted an escape from that. But people like Jane, who offered such escape from mundanity, were themselves in the center of the chaos. They were chain smoking. They were ditching school. They were unreliable narrators of their own story. They offered shards of truth, but there was no connection to anything sustainable, and of course the shards can cut you without any apology. And those shards glimmered, even underwater, to anyone who ever had a heart.

You stood there every day thinking you had to testify enough of your love, you had to raise yourself above the muck, you had to feel it hard enough, at which point an angel would shine their light and you and her would embark on the escalator to happiness together. Then you could finally serial kill or start a band, whatever made you happy.

You weren't around for the night when her friend fell out of the window and died. "How could this have happened?" You knew exactly how. You could trace the path she fell in each of your ribs. You knew how hard it is to hold onto someone who wants to drown. You knew how falling is the absolute, unmovable compass point of some people. As much as you try to wrestle the needle out of their hand, it's always pointing down.

Only later did you hear the original of the song and see how completely different it was as written by Lou Reed. The cover is underwater, while the original was on dry land. The cover is avoidant, indulgent, soppy wet with promises. The original was confrontational, funny, obtuse.

You were in the wrong version of the song.

You were in the right song, but the wrong version.

You were in a song.

You were a song.

SPEKTRUM

You open your eyes. You are still in that blue room, and now you wonder if somehow this one takes longer than the others. But that wouldn't be possible, because all the other rooms have someone in them, and those people all have to move at the same time, right? You are like train cars, all of you in your separate boxes.

You turn one of the letters on the device in front of you so that it now reads:

LOAD

There. You suppose that's progress.

You close your eyes again.

Somehow it all reversed. Your role in everything. You used to be unable to sink. But then there was that lake, years later. Amongst the thousands of lakes in the Midwest, there was a tiny one in South Dakota you stopped at with her. It was your route, you were driving, but it always felt like you were trailing her.

Somehow it flipped around. She used to be drowning, you were buoyant. And then she was the strong swimmer, and you couldn't stay afloat.

When you both ran out on the dock, she jumped in, right over the sign on the railing that said *NO DIVING*, and swam across. You tried to follow her as her burgundy hair bobbed across the blue water.

You dove in too, and the lake stretched out into an ocean. You tried to turn back but you were too far from the shore. It was such a small lake, really, as lakes go, but she was on the other side and, of course, drowning people don't look like they're drowning. There was no energy for screaming or even speaking. Even if she were six feet from you, she would barely notice anything wrong, because all your effort had to go into keeping your mouth above water. Your muscles were stiff, and you

SPEKTRUM

couldn't push through.

You were too far from land. The feeling that rushed into your body was one of embarrassment. *What a stupid way to die.* To just flail in a lake with nobody watching, not even her.

You thought you were maybe close enough for one final lunge to touch the shore, but when your foot hit nothing, you really felt like that could be it. Drowned in the smallest lake in South Dakota. What would she do after that? She didn't even know how to call your mother. Funny how the last thoughts can be of logistics: *What a mess this will make for everyone.*

But you did have one more kick in you, your big toe caught a clump of mud, and you were able to leverage your stiff body forward and onto the shore, where you collapsed, out of breath, looking up at the blue sky, feeling that mixture of relief and stupidity you always hope will lead to some changed behavior but you know probably won't.

Above you, the sky was the most serene blue. That whole episode was so quiet, including your struggle. You could almost have kept it a secret and no one would have known.

You looked up and saw her burgundy head bobbing back towards you, so you lay back on the mud, breathing deeply, grateful just to have air in your lungs instead of cold water.

After a minute, you looked up again to see if she had arrived, but in her place were six ducks, who had previously congealed in your blurry vision to look like her head. They quietly swam up to shore, spread out around you and walked up onto the beach. They navigated what was to you a dangerous expanse of water like they were a family stepping off a moving sidewalk at the airport.

In that moment, you thought either you had died,

and this was some kind of peaceful transition to a duck-filled heaven, or that she had died, and these were the avian messengers carrying an echo of her life across the lake.

Neither turned out to be true, as a minute later she came swimming across.

"I almost drowned," you said to her, after you finally caught your breath.

"Wait. Really?" she said.

How had your buoyancy changed so much? You want the world to stop and kneel down, to pray with you or hold you in those moments, but the world, its business far from over, doesn't share the same experience. The world subsumes everything eventually, every old duck and frail swimmer, and it would have subsumed your body, too.

Even as your bloated form would have been dredged

SPEKTRUM

out of the lake, even as she went through the trail of common friends in her phone to try to somehow locate your parents, there would still be the deep blue of the water that was always clear whenever you cupped some in your hands, there would be the ducks preening themselves, there would be the blue South Dakota sky that has witnessed much more tragic events than this.

You open your eyes again to the same blue room. Another turn of the dial and you have:

GOAD

Like the dial itself is speaking to you. Like it is saying, "Go on, you're almost there." Just one more nudge. You almost don't want to do it, because you feel like it's a grooved path, that there is only one direction to go. Why do you take the hand of a masked person as they lead you to the next room? Why are you so *trusting?*

SPEKTRUM

You want to turn away from everything. You feel like you can barely breathe. Maybe there's still some of that South Dakota water in your lungs.

You move the last dial into place:

G O L D

Your time in the blue room must have lasted double the length of the other rooms. They must have skipped you.

You take another deep breath in.

You hold it for a few seconds.

You exhale.

You decide to finally read the letter in front of you.

SPEKTRUM

For a while it hurt so much to lose you. To lose you before I even met you. But then I thought, that's what happened with the Big Trees. As soon as I found out they existed, I learned that nine out of every ten of them were already gone. But. There is one thing I have to say about this. There was a time on Earth before all of this. A time before even those great ancient forests existed. And. The time before the Big Trees was not sad. Somehow all this love burst forth out of nothing. All the trees grew larger than you could ever imagine. Where did they even get the notion? But they did. So. I just want to tell you. It can happen again. All we need is time. Which, thank God, is an illusion, after all.

SPEKTRUM

You take another deep breath and appreciate that, thank God, you are not underwater.

Finally, the woman with the white veil comes in to get you and lead you to the next room. You take off the headphones and set them down. You spin the dials to mix up the word again.

∞ ∞

I'm almost to the end of my story. I promise you this is all worth it.

John Dabrowiak's grandson Chester, my grandfather, was born in South Bend in 1912. He worked as a meatcutter and a taxidermist, married Evelyn in the local church in 1939, and in 1995 once visited me in the brief months when I was attending college in Monterey, California. Chester was very pleased to shake the hand of the pastor at San Juan Bautista Mission, where I was participating in an archeological dig and had found a mother-of-pearl cross in an old well. The cross meant nothing to me religiously, even though I came from a long string of ancestors who saw crosses every day, set into the brickwork of the buildings in their village, and who learned to read so that they could read the word of God. Chester himself went to church every Sunday, but the lineage of Christian faith in our family ended with his generation.

Chester's wife Evelyn died after a battle with Alzheimer's in 1996. As a child, I couldn't understand why she wanted to double-bolt the locks on the big solid wooden door when we went out to lunch, why she pressed her hands down against her dress to smooth it out with her gaunt brow knitted in fear.

Chester smiled easily, showed me how to have a strong handshake and take big strides when I walked. He never once spent a night in a hospital until he was eighty-eight. Since his death wasn't sudden, he most certainly would have arranged for a priest to issue the last rites.

SPEKTRUM

There was an odd chill in the air when I would go into his basement as a kid to look at the taxidermy animals he had stuffed, and the drawers full of eyes. What a strange transmutation that is, to give a creature life after death.

Chester once showed me a prayer card of his uncle Stanislaus, whose features looked exactly like mine, down to the hairline. It was like in a movie when they cast the same actor to play two separate generations. I was intrigued by the fact that it said on the back of the card that Stanislaus was born in South Bend, but died in Santa Fe, New Mexico in 1955.

Years later, on a trip through Santa Fe, I went into a library and asked to look at microfilm of the newspapers from 1955. The librarian showed me how to set up the reel by putting it on the machine. She spun it a little, and then zoomed in and focused on a random page. She just happened to have found, amongst all those newspaper pages, the exact spot where the obituary of my great-uncle Stanislaus was printed.

I learned from that article that, after living his whole life in Indiana, he decided to spend his last year in Santa Fe in the hope that it would ease the suffering of his tuberculosis.

SPEKTRUM

SPEKTRUM

INDIGO

[Focus.]

SPEKTRUM

SPEKTRUM

The veiled woman leads you to a four-poster bed with fog billowing all around it. The sheets are dyed indigo. You look at her. She gestures to you to lie down. As you do so, she sits next to you on the bed, angled away. She is in a vintage lacy white dress, and you feel like she is there to help you, but you are also not sure whether she is, you know, *alive*.

There are friendly ghosts, too, you think. *They just want to help.*

The good news would be that you are finally able to see ghosts.

But no, you saw her open a curtain a few minutes ago. She must be real. Perhaps she is praying. Maybe she is weeping.

You look up at a white scrim hanging above the bed. A film is being projected onto it, just for you. The first thing you see projected is a piece of indigo film stock with scratches on it, all of them jiggling frenetically.

SPEKTRUM

You remember the film projectors in elementary school, and how the films they projected were all hopelessly out of date and irrelevant to you, like propaganda for a forgotten war. They gave the impression of a world that was built with great fervor and sacrifice and then not further refined. Did everyone get tired?

Then you see the word *FOCUS* with multicolored circles all around it.

Then a picture of the redwoods through an indigo filter.

You hear piano music start to play. Tentatively at first. Just the stuttering middle C. Isn't that where everyone begins? It reminds you of your hesitating first moments on the piano back in the yellow salon.

Above you is footage of a bird stuck inside a building, trying to get through a window above the door.

SPEKTRUM

What is the word for the window above a door? A carapace, you want to say, but you know that's not right. Maybe that's the word for the frilly thing people used to wear around their necks. No, no, no. The bird doesn't see that someone has opened the door below her, which stays open for a few seconds and then closes again. She flies off, still trapped inside.

In between these scenes, film leader keeps counting down: 5—4—3—2 . . . It always stops at two and then goes black—or indigo, actually—and then another piece of film starts counting down again from somewhere higher: 8—7—6 . . . you can feel the change in eras just in these scraps of film. The design of the numbers in one will be clearly from the '50s and then it will be very '70s.

Another title card says *FOCUS*.

The woman in white is still sitting next to you. She hasn't moved. You almost want to peer over her shoulder and see what she's doing. It calms you to think that maybe she's mending something. That's what the man in the coyote mask did back in the kitchen. It's what made you feel you could trust him.

You hear the piano playing something soft and delicate. It sounds familiar, but you're not sure if it is just in the category of music that *sounds* familiar, or if the notes are actually part of some existing piece of music.

You once thought Chopin's "Prelude in E Minor" would be the music you'd want to hear on your deathbed. The way the chords descend feels like water meandering down rocks, both perfectly intuitive and turning corners on a whim. Then you fell in love with "Nessun Dorma" as sung by Luciano Pavarotti. It came on at least twice a night at the Napoleon House when you worked there as a busboy. Every night your right knee wobbled a bit as he hit that high note and it felt like the universe was tearing apart.

SPEKTRUM

Above you there is footage of a woman with a very fashionable haircut sitting on a stool. Just when the camera focuses on her, it cuts to indigo again.

Indigo now seems like a better black than black. It is the color of the Earth's atmosphere when it is slipping away into space, when you might start to fear that there's not enough oxygen to stay alive.

Slow down your breathing. Conserve your air.

That woman with the haircut looked familiar, but, like the music, you don't know if it's just that the kinds of women who are filmed sitting on stools tend to look very similar.

There are a few seconds of indigo, but the echo of that woman's face remains. Maybe the woman in white is veiled because she's that woman on the stool. Maybe she's veiled because she's no longer that woman.

SPEKTRUM

Maybe her task is indeed mending, but maybe you are what she is mending.

Indigo, you now remember, is a plant that is not colored indigo when it is alive. It is green and violet, and the deep blue has to be wrung out of it, almost like its blood is colored indigo, almost like it lives this covert life and then becomes something else.

We think of ancestry usually in human terms, but there is an ancestry in plants. The scents of rosemary and lavender are like family recipes handed down for generations. What would it even mean for a plant to break off from that lineage, assert their independence, move to the mountains and take a tech job? What would it mean if someone picked up a sprig of rosemary, broke it apart and held it to their nose to smell that familiar scent, and there was nothing there? What does our drive for independence rob us of?

You see footage of a man as he runs across a plank,

away from a giant redwood tree with a big wedge cut into it. You realize that the tree is falling over and that this man is the one who sawed into it. He is rather serene for how big this tree is, but he knows that he cut it in such a way that it will fall away from him. The film cuts to indigo before the tree crashes down.

If someone had a lot of material wealth and they wanted to fight against magic—the magic of forests and medicine and cultural wisdom—the only way to do it would be to destroy the people practicing it and discredit its very existence. At first, they would have to start out very aggressively, killing anyone they suspected of being a witch.

And the lineage of that genocide would be a deeply embodied fear. If someone has done the heavy work of genocide early on, their descendants can reinforce that fear with the smallest of actions. When it gets all the way down to you, hundreds of years later, you don't even need all the hatred in your heart to maintain that oppression. You've become an ancestral appendage to a lineage of fear. You are enacting the later acts of a play, and you're not even aware of it.

So, they built a culture of forgetting. Everyone born must learn to forget. It is a culture of invisibility. They cannot let people know the power that is sparkling all around them. It is too dangerous. They ridiculed it. They degraded feminine and sensitive traits so much that no one would want to be painted with such a brush, especially those raised to be men. "Well, I don't want to be woo-woo."

A large crowd of people is on the beach and rhythmically pounding the water so that a great big turbid frothing appears. The image passes by so quickly that you can't possibly understand what is going on.

Absolute knowledge is colonial in nature. It is commensurate with the naming of places that already had names, the damming of rivers, the corralling of people, the silencing of their cultures. The imagined endgame is some sort of ultimate trivia contest where knowing the exact distance from the Earth to the Moon gets you all the praise you could have hoped for.

Absolute knowledge is for absolute power. It consolidates information so it can be controlled. Relative knowledge liberates people. It allows them to have control over their own lives by seeing the patterns and symmetries in which we are all enmeshed.

There is a stumble in the piano notes and that's when you realize this isn't a recording you're listening to. This isn't preexisting music. This is someone in the yellow room playing the piano right now, making mistakes. Just like you were.

Someone is comforting the dying.

Are you the dying?

SPEKTRUM

You want to jump up, but the woman in white is sitting there, and you don't want to upset her. You feel like you should stay and keep watching the film above you. You wish all your friends were here.

You squirm in your bed as the film above shows a blueprint of some piece of machinery flapping in a light breeze. So many things to build, so many plans, so many parts to cut out, grind down, fit together.

How did you end up on your deathbed? You took all the steps you were supposed to take. You woke up. You dressed in black. You drove through a red light. You sat alone in a room and thought of drowning. And now you are here, lying on this bed, looking up at a cartoon squadron of bomber jets flying over the sea. Propaganda for a forgotten war.

But it was all connected, everything you walked through. You didn't really believe it when the letter said to play like you were comforting the dying, and now you realize that it's too late, that you should have taken that assignment more seriously. It's just that you've been lied to so many times about so many things.

The woman in the veil is sitting with you through all this. Wordlessly. Gesturelessly. Her back is turned towards you, but you can feel her love. A love that beams in all directions.

Why were you too cool for God? God is a love that extends beyond any personal interest. It is a person sitting with you while you die.

Tears crest in your eyes.

The woman in white does this with everyone, you realize. Every day. This doesn't cheapen the meaning but intensifies it. How does she have the patience to just sit there? She sits while people search through their memories and realize what they're doing here in this indigo bed, softly weeping at images of so many things:

The sun shining through a dark indigo sky, the grain of the film illuminated like dents in stainless steel.

Clouds moving quickly overhead.

The camera moving slowly through a redwood forest. An indigo-hued forest. As though the little indigo plants figured out the trick to catching sunlight that the redwoods learned long ago:

Build your own home.

Live inside yourself.

Be patient.

Stay still.

Allow the fire to envelop you.

SPEKTRUM

Allow people to chop into you and walk away smiling as you fall down, two thousand years cut down in a matter of minutes. Even as 95 percent of your friends are removed from around you, you don't shout, you don't fight back, you don't write protest songs. You just stand there.

Absolute knowledge tells you that your participation in something doesn't matter.

And then it's set. They can keep that order of the material world, of absolute knowledge, with a simple eye roll at the dinner table. That eye roll tells someone that curiosity and intuition are unacceptable. There is no discussion to have.

Now you can see how your ancestors might have tricked you. They said that the debt wouldn't be overwhelming. That you should take out a loan for a house. That you should stick it out in a difficult marriage because *what do you think, marriage is supposed to be easy?*

They all led you astray with a loving touch, when at times the best thing they could have done was nothing.

Nothing.

Nothing.

Sparks of fire are rising from the bottom of the frame, the fire itself unseen. Indigo sparks, so we know this fire is really hot.

Again, the film leader counts down, never reaching one.

5—4—3—2 . . .

The piano music is the most beautiful music you've ever heard. If you could choose your deathbed music, it would be this, exactly as it's playing now, with all the stumbles and pauses and doubts. Everything is more perfect this way than if it had been rehearsed and refined. Perfection is too overwhelming.

You realize that you'll never meet the person who is playing the music while you are dying.

For the first time you notice another instrument playing. You were so focused on the piano that you thought this other sound was just an echo. But it's an electric guitar. It's matching the piano, playing off it. And again, the only time you notice that it's human is when there is a mistake. A little flub of a note, something misplaced. This means that someone was playing guitar along with you, too. Even when you thought you were alone, you were being echoed.

More scratched film leader, like an animation made from the scraps of a bombed-out building.

More slow-motion footage moving through a redwood forest. You keep peeking behind every indigo redwood to see if someone is there. You almost want the redwoods to fight back at some point. After so many lines are sent forth to their slaughter and yet nothing changes in the machinery of destruction, you almost want a tree to fight back.

But it never does. And there is no defeating someone who refuses to fight.

You hear another kind of music, separate from the piano and the guitar. Chimes playing in that dreamy ascending way again. You know your time is done.

Another film leader comes on. This one looks like it's from the '80s.

5—

What year did they stop making film countdowns like this? The veiled woman on the bed stands up.

4—

SPEKTRUM

Surely they don't make them anymore. When was the last time you saw a film countdown? She turns around and offers her hand.

3—

What does it matter? It's gone now. You sit up.

2—

She opens a curtain and leads you through it.

The light is so much brighter than you ever imagined.

∞ ∞

My father Richard was born in South Bend in 1944. He paid for college at Purdue University with a paper route, married Carol in a church in Chicago, took a job as an engineer in Sacramento, California, and raised me and my brother in a nice house near the river. Somehow our family didn't maintain any traditions, recipes, songs, or stories of my ancestors. I don't even know when they died out. There were no prayers of gratitude for all the work Jakub did to build prosperity for his family. There was no awareness of the journey Nepomucyn took across the Atlantic Ocean so that we could all have a life in the United States. Somehow those stories didn't stay alive.

After Chester died, his house was sold, his possessions given away. I inherited his car, a Ford Tempo. As I drove it down the spine of the country, I stopped at a little rest stop with swaying willow trees. As I was about to get out, I saw something glinting near the rearview mirror. It was a little metal token sewn into the interior of the car's roof, as though it had evaded a search to remove all personal items. I undid the stitch and looked at this faded medallion. It was a portrait of Saint Christopher, the patron saint of travel.

SPEKTRUM

SPEKTRUM

SPEKTRUM

VIOLET

[ ]

SPEKTRUM

SPEKTRUM

You step through the curtain into a violet room. You look like you've been crying.

There is a hanging lantern beaming a golden light, surrounded by twisting branches, like something from a fairy tale. Their shadows spiral outward. A little table with a golden tablecloth holds a tea kettle. On the wall there is a painting of a starling bursting out of a rainbow.

At the table is a man dressed in white, holding a black, hollow-bodied electric guitar and waiting for the water to boil. This is me.

Hello.

You can take a seat on the golden couch there. In a minute I'll serve you a cup of tea.

I've been in this room the whole time, trying to reach you. I have a little notebook where I write down my experiences of trying to play guitar along with people as they struggle with the piano in the yellow salon. In a minute, you'll hear the next person's fragile attempts come out of these speakers. I spend my time here guessing at the nature of their character based solely on how they approach the piano, and I write down descriptions like:

Lively.

Wistful.

Defiant.

They can hear me too, but they usually don't realize I'm a person. Every night it's like I'm trying to communicate from beyond the grave. At first, I thought my job was to match people's piano playing as best I could and harmonize with them. Then I tried to echo their notes. But I soon realized that the more perfectly I was able to play along with them, the less human I must have seemed.

I tried to think of all the things a computer would never do. I played a note while detuning it. I rubbed my fingernail lightly against the string. I played in jagged rhythms, first in time and then out of time. How do you wake someone up from a dream when you are also in the dream, but in the next room? How do you convince someone that they're not alone? Sometimes nothing works, and people play on without considering me. But every once in a while, I can tell I've gotten through to them. They stop playing and listen. I offer a little melody. They respond. We merge and harmonize, and it is so lovely. All this before I get to see anyone's faces, before I know anything at all about them.

Here is your cup of tea. I hope it gives you a moment to think about all that we've been through.

Every ten minutes the chimes ring and I go to the curtain to let someone in the room and gesture for them to sit on the couch. Just like you right now. I sit down and pour a cup of chamomile-rose tea.

SPEKTRUM

Those two tisanes merge into a beautiful color, like someone poured gold into a cup.

I set it down in front of the person and drink one myself to prove my trustworthiness. But I don't make eye contact. I want people to have the space to reflect on what they've been through without influence from me.

And then, always a couple minutes into the ten-minute cycle, I hear a tentative middle C over the speakers, and I offer a gentle response on my guitar. Nothing to overwhelm them at first. It's amazing how everyone plays something, regardless of whether they think they are a piano player or not. That letter really does the trick: *You're the best piano player in the room.*

Just last night, something amazing happened in this room. A woman was sitting on the couch, right where you are, when the chimes rang to signal the change of rooms. Usually, the person on the couch leaves the room before the next person comes through the curtain, but she took her time getting up and encountered the next person as he was entering the room. To dispel the awkwardness, the woman gave the man a hug. Perhaps they knew each other already, perhaps not. But because everyone is always so intent on learning "the rules" of how to behave, it set a precedent in this man's mind that this was what he should do upon leaving: hug the next person.

And so, without my intervention at all, a hug train began. I could barely contain my glee as I watched this develop. Could something so small take over the world? Could a renewal of basic kindness and love spread from this little building in the Santa Cruz Mountains and have a real impact on the well-being of humanity? Who knows what is possible.

It was like a microcosm of how traditions start: someone makes a sincere gesture, and everyone falls in line, wanting to do what they're supposed to do. Do the people following along enjoy the ritual as much, given that they "have to" do it? Or does it mean more to them because it connects them to a lineage?

After a few changeovers, people were still hugging the next person on their way out. I wondered if I had any responsibility to help maintain it. Could I subtly nudge people into this interaction? It started so effortlessly, and it continued so effortlessly, I was just happy to witness it. I carried on with my duties with even more focus than before: serve the tea, listen for the middle C, try to make it clear that I was a human being, alive in a body, wanting the best for the world.

I stayed out of the way of the chain of hugs, but with a side-glance I would regard the two people as they continued it. The effect was so profound, as though the woman who started it were hugging people all down the way into the future. A person being hugged through space and time: maybe that's what our friend Olivia meant by God?

This happened a half dozen times, and then, one time the chimes rang and a man got up from the couch and another man came from behind the curtain. Until now there had been at least one woman in every interaction. The new man didn't know what to expect, but the one who had been there knew what he was supposed to do. He had been hugged when he entered this room, and he was to give a hug upon leaving. That was how it worked, since as long as anyone could remember. You were a part of a long chain of hugs. Don't break the chain. Why would you want to?

But in this case, the man hesitated. He looked at the other man and stepped aside. He left without giving a hug.

And, just like that, the hug chain was broken. There was no way to reinstitute it, no "Hey remember when?" No revivals, no rebirths. I was crushed. I couldn't believe it ended. It had seemed like it could go on forever.

But I had to carry on. The next person came, and I served them tea and I played my guitar. I just had to keep going. I didn't let on that I was sad.

When you were in the yellow salon playing piano, I wrote down this one word: "Distressed." I tried to picture what you might be like just from the sound of those notes. Now that I see you in person, I can't even remember what it was I pictured. But I think the cups of chamomile-rose tea we are both drinking allow us a chance to not worry so much about identity.

I've been a bit distressed myself, to be honest. The other day I had an argument on the phone with my father. There is no explanation I can give for why the argument got so heated, but it was ostensibly about a car and where I parked it. I'm sorry to say

SPEKTRUM

I hung up on my dad, the only time I've ever done that. My mother texted afterwards apologizing for his anger, which was very nice of her. But I was afraid that my father and I wouldn't ever resolve it for real, and that, like the broken hug train, it would be up to two men to bridge an emotional divide and it just wouldn't happen.

Maybe that's how family traumas are buried. Nobody wants to bring them up at the next dinner, they are never written down or catalogued in any way, and they just become a nervous energy in someone's hands as they press down on their dress to smooth it out. What a lost opportunity there.

I wanted something more from this exchange with my dad, but how do you reach out to someone to ask for an apology without making it worse? Sometimes it's easier to talk to the dead than the living, so I went to my father's mother, Evelyn, who died of Alzheimer's. I hoped that she wouldn't think of me as just the impossibly shy child with glasses too big for his face. I hoped she would see my family as a continuation of all that her family had worked for.

I pictured her across the veil, uncontacted by her descendants, her pain and loss ignored. Perhaps that disease is a rebellion by the body to take away access to memories that are too painful, and it leaves a person in a spiral of forgetting until they forget that they are alive, and they spin off from an unbearable existence into the void. And even when the burdens of the body are eased, is there someone in the afterlife to help them understand what happened, or at least to tell them that it wasn't their fault?

And so, one fall day, twenty-five years after her death, I endeavored to talk to my grandmother Evelyn again.

I had never tried contacting a deceased person. I didn't know what to do other than carry her in my thoughts throughout the day. I went to the farmer's market and looked for zucchini and kale and I pictured her next to me.

"This is kale," I said to Evelyn, "one of those new trendy foods that you might be confused by. It's like lettuce but rougher and more bitter. People always make fun of me for liking it so much, but I think you just need to know how to prepare it. You can't digest it very well in its original form. You have to have some of the digestion happen outside of your body. You can do that with vinegar or salt or heat. Just find ways of softening the kale so it can enter your body and not be such a shock. Why do we even bother with such a tough and bitter vegetable? Well, because it brings us the light and energy of the sun. It brings us so many nutrients that will skip around in our body and bring life and hope. You know this. It wants to heal us. It loves us and wants us to be alive."

I came home from the farmer's market and made dinner for my wife. I thought of the vegetables and the local meats, and the lives those beings led that brought them to our home.

Then, after dinner, as my wife lay down to sleep, I took a notebook and sat at the kitchen table. I lit a couple of candles, softened my gaze, and thought about Evelyn. Most of this process felt very similar to the creative process, so similar, in fact, that I had to let go of needing to delineate truth from fiction. Who can tell exactly when blue turns into indigo?

The lights were off. My computer and phone were in a separate room. The candles flickered. I took out a pen and wrote a question to Evelyn. Very loose and slow, just asking if she was around. Like you do when you sit at a piano, and you let your hands find their own way and see if there is a tune to be found.

After I finished my question, my hand went to the next line and wrote a response, and I kept asking questions and writing the responses. There was never any thought or deliberation. I didn't strain to come up with words or consider what she would say. I expressed my gratitude for my grandmother, and she expressed her gratitude to me for listening. I asked her how she was feeling, what she needed. I told her I was sorry she was in pain.

We talked for maybe ten minutes, and I knew I was done because it felt like there was a subtle change in the air pressure. I set down my pen and cried. I would try more conversations with her in the future, I decided, and I wouldn't need to know who exactly was moving my pen, and whether it was like the intuition you need to write fiction, or whether it was actually her spirit in the room with me.

This felt different, though, because I never cry during the writing process. They were tears of gratitude, almost like an alchemical process had occurred.

The next day—out of the blue, as they say—my father texted. He apologized for our argument. I hadn't told him about my conversation with Evelyn.

SPEKTRUM

What I'm saying is I want you to imagine that, after your own death, you become a spirit. You live still, in a way, in between the walls, or across an inexplicable divide, and you can still see the people you love. But you are dead. And you realize how much more you love them because now you are unable to touch them or make them laugh or eat popcorn together. And you just want to tell them thank you I'm sorry thank you I'm sorry thank you.

Some people will say, "I don't know, I don't believe in that woo-woo stuff." While you, the spirit, are standing right there, a formless, bodiless, ghost wishing you could taste a satsuma orange again and feel the juice drip down your wrist. You cringe because you are that woo-woo stuff they don't believe in. You are the mystery in a book that they have closed without reading. You are the puzzle that has too many pieces, and your loved ones, your family, your own children say, "I don't get it. It's too hard."

But then, what if just one of them says, "Well, I'll

SPEKTRUM

just try to listen. I'll sit here and light a candle and see, and maybe . . . well, I don't know."

Imagine you, the ghost, standing there, unable to talk with those you love so much, unable to tell them, "It's okay, everything you go through, it's okay. I love your voice when you hum to yourself as you're pouring tea, and I love the way you pull your sleeves over your hands."

You aren't able to say any of that because you're on the other side, so you're only able to make the candle flicker, or maybe get the cat to prick his ears up, or swing the gate back and forth and make it squeal. But you know that you are still real.

And someone says, "Oh, that? No, that's just the gate. That's just the cat being weird. Candles flicker all the time, that's what they do."

But your avenues of expression are so limited that you only have candles and cats and gates.

SPEKTRUM

You can't send a text message.

You can't grab someone by the arm.

You know only this: everyone you love, living and dead, is still real. You will go to such great lengths to reach them. You will cross impossible wilderness, long blue lakes. If the spirits could get the living to do just one thing for them, it would be to try to listen.

Ah, there's that chime again. I feel so close to you because it seems like we have so much in common. I hope you know that you're going to be okay.

You take one last look around the room. You breathe deep and step outside. The door closes behind you and you are on the street again. Cars drive past. A truck revs its engine. Two people in conversation walk by. The sky isn't completely black. It still has a little bit of purple in it. You look all around you for a crow, but now there aren't any in sight.